INNER AND OUTER LANDSCAPES

A Collection of Modern Poetry

Susanne Rowell

The characters and events portrayed in this book are fictitious. Any similarity to real persons, living or dead, is coincidental and not intended by the author.

No part of this book may be reproduced, or stored in a retrieval system, or transmitted in any form or by any means, electronic, mechanical, photocopying, recording, or otherwise, without express written permission of the publisher.

Front Cover: Painting, Acrylic on Canvas,

'The idea of New York'

Copyright © 2023 Susanne Rowell

All rights reserved.

ISBN:-9798388213136

DEDICATION

For my mother

To Anna

Susanne Proulx

CONTENTS

	Acknowledgments	1
	OUTER LANDSCAPES	2
1	Oxford 1987	3
2	Austria 1975	4
3	On the moor again	5
4	Bridge across the river	6
5	Italian Holiday	7
6	The last day of the holiday	8
7	In Finistère	9
8	Dinan, Brittany	10
9	Uncommon Verses Trilogy I-II	11
9	Uncommon Verses Trilogy III	12
10	American Way of Life	13
11	Ultima Thule, Spitsbergen	14
12	Selfoss/Iceland	15
13	The Geese in Hesperia Park	16
14	Ancient City of Desire	17
	IN-BETWEEN LANDSCAPES	18
15	Seawards – Alone I	19
15	Seawards – Alone II	20
15	Seawards – Alone III	21

15	Seawards – Alone IV	22
15	Seawards – Alone V	23
16	Novel-Ghost-Town	24
17	Day-Trip to the Moon	25
18	Storm over the Lake	26
19	Sentiments, Gathered	27
19	Sentiments, Gathered	28
20	Afternoon in the park	29
21	Garden Path	30
22	Walking towards the Windmill	31
22	Walking towards the Windmill	32
23	Of the things you do not see	33
24	Bologna	34
25	Cervo, Alassio	35
26	Memories. destroyed	36
26	Memories, destroyed	37
27	Small Town, Passing	38
28	It happened on an ordinary day	39
28	It happened on an ordinary day	40
29	Cover their cages	41
29	Cover their cages	42
30	Guide dogs for the blind	43
31	Inlet	44

32	Misconception	45
	INNER LANDSCAPES	46
33	Don Quixote is dead	47
34	The Empty Place	48
34	The Empty Place	49
34	The Empty Place	50
35	Dreamwalk	51
36	The Eternal Puzzle	52
36	The Eternal Puzzle	53
37	The last time I saw your face	54
38	As man, as horse	55
39	I will die on a Wednesday	56
39	I will die on a Wednesday	57
40	New Morning	58
41	Chance Meeting	59
42	Escapology	60
43	Newsroom@Horror.com	61
44	Anger	62
45	Belisha-Cindy	63
46	Vacancy	64
46	Vacancy	65
47	Equinox	66
48	Inside the Observatory	67

49	Destiny, Revisited	68
50	High-Way-Love-Prayer	69
51	The Place Everyone knows	70
52	One Afternoon	71
53	Soul-Chrysalides	72
54	At Peace, At Last	73
55	Dead Man's Bench	74
56	Wrong Turn	75
57	In Lancashire	76
57	In Lancashire	77
58	The 79	78
59	Ad Infinitum	79
60	Wake Of the Dead	80
61	The Arrival	81
62	Grandmother	82
62	Grandmother	83
63	My Treasure Without Compare	84
64	Daughter Nature	85
65	Fear Made of Fish	86
66	Promenade with Magritte	87
67	De Chirico's Dream	88
68	The Keepers of Time	89
68	The Keepers of Time	90

69	Fantasia Faunus	91
69	Fantasia Faunus	92
70	Time	93
70	Time	94
71	Night Flight	95
72	Hour of Deliverance	96
73	Unnoticed	97

ACKNOWLEDGMENTS

Thanks go to my husband Jonathan and my good friend Leslie for their ongoing support, encouragement, copy-reading, and advice.

OUTER LANDSCAPES

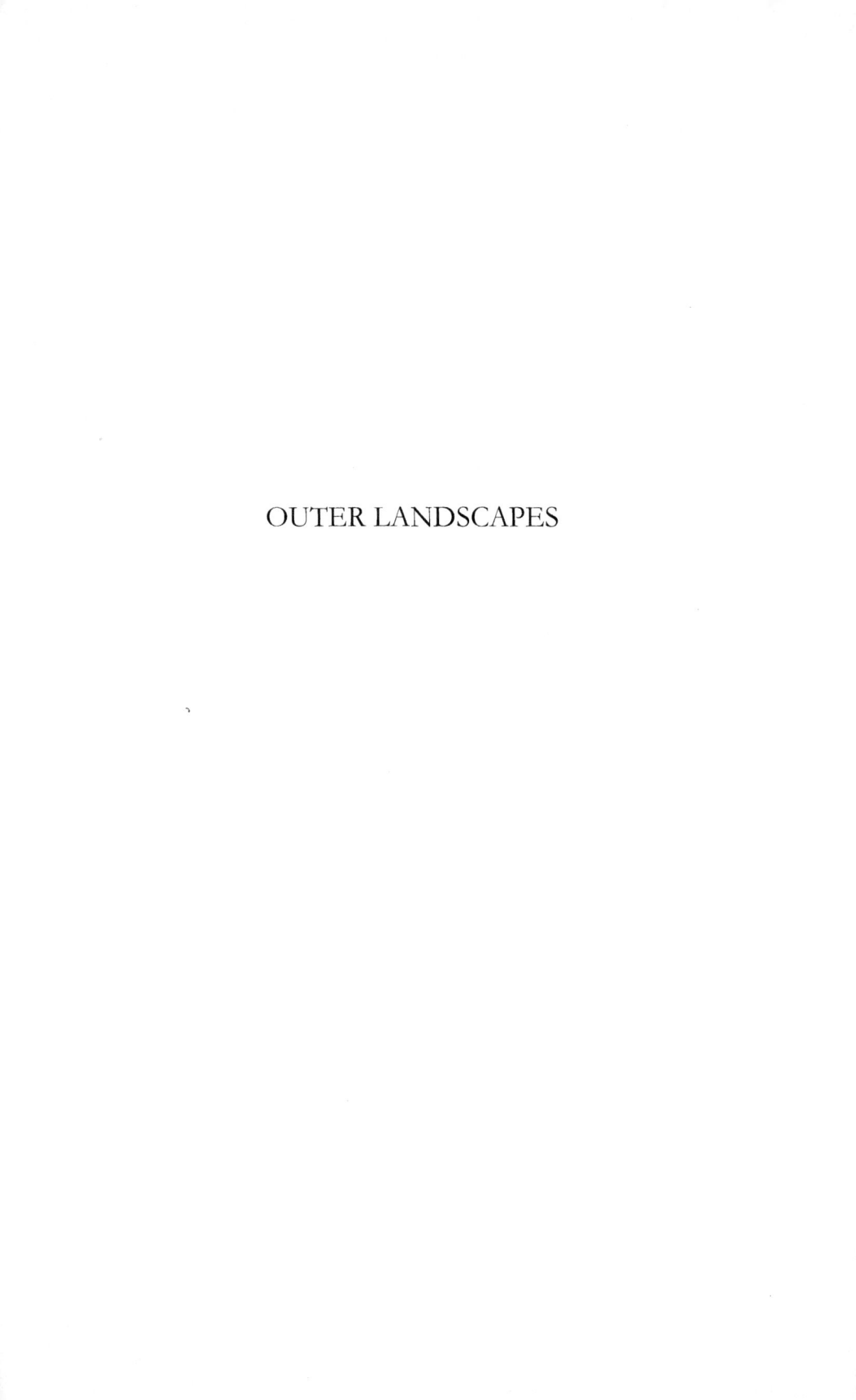

OXFORD 1987

Oarsmen practicing for that famous race,
the memory is lodged crystal-clear in my mind,
of a summer's day and countless more like it.

A cheer, a wave, a floating scene,
a moment in time, as I ambled along
the green banks of Cherwell River.

The way the crinkly shower cap felt,
how it contrasted with the soap wrapper's
smoothness, in the hotel's bathroom,

in the morning, before I went downstairs,
for breakfast, where the air smelled
of fire-wood, and sunrays illuminated

dancing dust particles along their path
through bull's-eye window panes.
Sitting between crooked oak beams,

my stomach lurching with nervous tension,
God only knows why, you said, and I couldn't
explain it, for I didn't understand myself.

Later on, I was transformed, into the essence
of curiosity and freedom, amidst the cobblestone,
the knick-knack shops and tea rooms.

My hair, still long and blond back then,
moved by a breeze, and I imagined, how the
afternoon's sunlight must have shone on it,

when the boy, not more than sixteen,
touched it, giggling, admiringly, in a
shy kind of way, saying *it feels so soft*.

AUSTRIA 1975

As we walked downhill, I could see where the
snowmelt had cut a path into the mountainside.
A gravel bed, now sprouting with flowers. Above it,
a sky so fresh and blue with white clouds, as if
an artist had just painted them - oils and pastels,
lush brushstrokes on canvas. The chairlift travelling
overhead, children's feet dangling carefree in thin air.

Close to the timberline, woodchucks were playing
on alpine pastures, the afternoon's sun adding
an auburn shine to their dense fur. A postcard kitsch
landscape, red and yellow coloured plastic chairs
outside a mountain restaurant, the likes I haven't seen
since. Come to think of it, nothing has quite looked the
same, not after we received that phone call.
It was back then, that I learned never to trust a sunny day.

ON THE MOOR AGAIN

I found myself there again,
where the opening unwinds
old stories-
your father is dead.

Wild ponies and rocks,
heather amongst granite,
gorse squeezing
memories tight.

It is then, that I remember
the hot air balloon,
balancing effortlessly
over ancient burial grounds.

Your voice; Walking, clambering.
The mist clinging onto the stream, tight,
lingering around the askant oak tree,

its protruding roots,
fingers pointing towards
our future lives.

BRIDGE ACROSS THE RIVER

We sat on the sandy beach,
the grassland behind, herbal scent,
skin burnt, eyes squint
against the sunshine.

The river travelled along calmly,
that Sunday afternoon,
gurgling carefree in our ears,
transcending underneath the bridge.

Longing for the cooling depth,
we swam around in circles;
A duck sailed by with ease and grace,
at home in its seesaw world.

Then, just as we dried ourselves,
we heard it, a faint splash,
not much to attract attention;
a pebble hitting the water's surface.

It was later at home,
while listening to the radio,
in the afterglow of heat,
drinking Orange and Lemonade,
that we learned about the man,

who was found, downstream,
on the sandbank,
where a sharp bend
changes the river's direction,
completely.

ITALIAN HOLIDAY

That first night, I dreamt,
that I was still at home,
between scents of
cherry blossom, and
owl hoots.

The motion of the car
was still with me,
and your breathing
felt unfamiliar in the dark.

I thought of us as lions, sleeping
in the heat of an African Savanna.

How many people have
stayed in this house before?
How many moons have
risen above this village?

The saturated air was streaming
through the wooden shutters,
*no need to close the windows
at night*, you said, *there shouldn't
be any mosquitos up in the mountains.*

A drunkard returned home from the tavern.
There was red wine in his song.
A woman's voice yelled from inside a house.
The crickets chirped in the grass.

I lay awake and listened to their stories.

THE LAST DAY OF THE HOLIDAY

came ablaze in a shower of light,
like the time it takes for an idea
to surface on the dumbstruck mind.
All along the winding road
the villages told of loneliness,
as if the olive trees
were withered signposts
in a bleached-out land
and a secret command
had told them to reassemble
in a hopeless pattern,
following a hidden code,
when with a sudden jolt,
the charm was broken,
as the boy on the motorcycle
caused you to stand on the brake
in a split second.

IN FINISTÈRE

We foraged
where the bramble hedges grew-
prickly companions

Craned our necks
balanced collecting bowls
found in our holiday kitchen

A saturated summer's breeze
skipped over Sinbad's ocean
while surfers dared meter-high waves

Never again did a blackberry crumble
taste this good

Of seawater
freedom
and old pirate stories

DINAN, BRITTANY

As I stroll through the old town,
marvelling at its skew-whiff buildings,
I suddenly become aware, that I've been talking
to you for a while – in my mind.

I've pointed out floral displays, a lit up art gallery, a limping dog.
This feels good, so I shall continue.

As I sit down in the window of a Brasserie,
I find myself sharing the view with you,
commenting on late afternoon shoppers, hastening home.

An elderly lady, baguette tucked under one arm,
three kids, school-bags on their backs,
pushing each other along, in a playful way.

Two businessmen, lost in their own importance,
self-conscious of their expensive suits.

A group of pigeons, picking breadcrumbs
underneath the tables and chairs, stacked up for winter.

Finally, the two young lovers, holding hands,
walking side by side, eyes interlocked.
She is wearing a grey, woollen scarf with matching hat,
his jeans hang loose on long legs.

In the distance, behind them, the children's carrousel,
a nostalgic Merry-Go-Round:
Horses, swans and sleighs bopping up and down,
round and round, to a faint, yet familiar melody.

UNCOMMON VERSES TRILOGY
A TRIBUTE TO THE PHOTOGRAPHS
OF STEPHEN SHORE

I
Saskatchewan dirt track
Liquor store, way back
Barbershop in New Mexican sunlight
Bus Stop next to surreal cacti

Endless heaven, California Bay
Motel sign, dusty highway
Pickup truck at Terrace Bay
Grand impressions, Cinemascope Day

New York bargains, Moody Maine
Wallstreet Journal, more to gain
Fast Food Restaurant, do eat more
Horseshoe Motel, welcomes all

II
Woman's World with Mannequin
Plastic dream in blue
Gold blond wig with sixties chic
Paramount flick, peroxide trick

Tyrone Cutter, Hairstyle smooth
Corner of a Diner Booth
Hobbs Lamp Lighter, Holiday Inn
Golden Nugget, small-town sin

El Paso Street
with tired feet
stormy site
and desert light

III
Sambo's Restaurant
Schellsburg P.A.
Post Card, Harrisburg
Time to stay

Boca Bayou
Navy Store
Amarillo
Time to go

Author's note: a reference to the wonderful photographs
'Uncommon Places' by Stephen Shore

AMERICAN WAY OF LIFE

Arizona, Motel Blues
Elvis Presley, Blue Suede Shoes
General Electric, Silver State
Mexican Light Zone
Hacienda's Gate

Epic Arrival, Phoenix Fades
Miracle Mile Strip, Tuscon State
Palm tree polaroid
Maple tree paranoid

Castaneda Shamen meets Matt Damon

ULTIMA THULE, SPITSBERGEN

Polar shadows of the past,
now layers in slate grey,
the northern sky, melting blue,
white icebergs passing through.

The rusty ships, forlorn,
an outpost in decay,
at the end of coal-town world,
at Pyramiden to stay.

Old-glory-signs, *Museum, Bar*
Lenin's head keeps guard,
the glacier cold, the town a ghost,
empty, melancholic heart.

Author's note: Spitsbergen is the largest island of the archipelago of the same name in the Arctic Ocean, which belongs to Norway. It is the only permanently inhabited island in the archipelago.

Pyramiden is a now abandoned and uninhabited Russian mining settlement. Ultima Thule is a mythical place, the northernmost part of the earth or universe to which one can travel. It is also part of many legends. Source: Wikipedia

SELFOSS/ICELAND

Trolls jinxed into stone cliffs
Along our path in the rain
The river's bed is a delta
For ancient myths to regain
The Vikings have not scarred this place
The ice just pretends to be blue
More along the lines of an illusion
A familiar lie, yet, strangely true

THE GEESE IN HESPERIA PARK

Now that it is July and the days are long
I will take the ferry out to Harakka Island,

to sit on its sloping green
- the colour of your eyes -

Do you remember what the sky looked like,
when the rain came towards the harbour?

The tram takes me past the city centre,
away from the geese in their thousands.

Mysteriously, the moonlight plays on
a dark iron-cast construction.

Within old walls, a lamp is lit.
What strange reconnaissance is this?

I hesitate, then walk on,
laughing at the absurdity
of the disappointment,
that dwells within.

Look, the geese have flown away.

ANCIENT CITY OF DESIRE

Chateaubriand
in your cold grave,
out in Saint-Malo Bay.

As waters gush
round your stony tomb,
seagulls screech
a forgotten prayer.

My feet are weary,
my soul flies,
my eyes feast
on your sight,

and ghostly
the moonlight illuminates,
the clouds
on this autumn night.

Along the Ramparts
of the Old Citadel,
a few tourists
are walking by.

Then we drive away
in our modern car,
but something inside my heart
is beginning to die.

IN-BETWEEN LANDSCAPES

SEAWARDS – ALONE

I

In the morning
I am split down the middle
From too much that is left unsaid

There and then the wave
Carries me along its crest
Of everyday talk

Effortlessly on your part

It amazes me how casually
Things can be mentioned

Like china stacked up
On a shelf

II

There is no reason
Why the cling clang
Of a spoon

In the ocean
Of my coffee
Should remind me

Of the ropes
On moored
Sailboats

Down at the harbour

III

Maybe this implies
Departure, broken hearts,
Goodbyes

Like the old stone tower
Standing guard at
The end of the bay

I know-
Later in the day
Memories will surface

Goldfish trapped in my brain bowl

IV

Was it your voice?
Or what you said?

I try to forget who I am
I try to remember what
I read about the old days
I conjure up images

Of daring buccaneers, Cape Horners'
Discovering new worlds
Trying to feel long-dead people's
Emotions. Surrogate pain.

Adventurous sailors
Emulating their toughness
How cold it must have been
Back then

And how the saltwater
Must have burned their skins

A thousand tears of ocean spray

V

All those stories
That have been
Confided

Pocketed snapshots
For later, to be taken out,
To be scrutinized

One by one

Instagrams of those twitters
The book I have to face
On my own-

Alone.

NOVEL-GHOST-TOWN

Been pacing through the idea of New York again,
page after page, across Brooklyn Bridge.

Sat at the diner on the corner of 8th street,
long-lost folly of my unconscious mind.

Followed the cryptic paths of the red notebook,
to the shabby Chinese stationery shop.

Deciphering Auster-SyncroniCity,
spaced out, inside my Moon Palace mind.

This literally tops reality from foretime,
when I strolled past these landmarks, block after block.

Stopped at the edge of Hudson River,
to notice the ghost of my yesterday self.

As it failed to recognize its future incarnation,
I returned to the apartment of a thousand books.

Author's note: This poem is dedicated to the books of
Paul Auster.
A German language version of this poem was published
in 'Poesie 21, Aal, Beet, Zeh, Lesen & Schreiben, Gedichte
Anthologie, Verlag Steinmeier'

DAY TRIP TO THE MOON

At dawn, we'll take the elevator to the moon,
have breakfast in lit-up lunar canteen.
The Crater-Express leaves stellar haven at ten,
for a scenic round-trip over the plain.
Promise, you'll hold my hand,
when our emerald world
starts to rise in the sunshine,
of the dark morning sky.

STORM OVER THE LAKE

The breeze edges its way across the water's surface,
the sky is made of fish-scale-grey.

A tree of lightning branches out, across the horizon,
illuminating the hotel room – electric white -

casting Kafkaesque shadows of interior objects
- a vase assuming preposterous dimensions -

up onto the ceiling and the walls.

While I stand on the balcony, leaning against
the weather-beaten iron railing, I am so grateful

for the sharpness of the storm, creasing the lake's skin,
into endless ripples.

Now that you're gone, I couldn't stand
the sight of the water's smoothness.

SENTIMENTS, GATHERED

Whatever happened to those old love songs?
My 'Angel Baby' and 'A Thousand Stars'.

To tinsel drape limousines?
A storybook, close to your heart.

Do you remember Rock 'n' Roll?
Paperboy skipping down the lane.

Love Chapel and the Book of Love,
the way that soda used to taste?

Sweet puppy love suburbia,
pink bubble gum of sentiments.

The desert's song, silently sung,
never to fade in our time.

Those beautiful convertibles,
Sixties celluloid sublime.

What happened to past future dreams?
Perfection staged with loving charms.

Whatever happened to those boys and girls?
Dense woods, clear lakes and summer days?

Dragged off by time's relentless pull.
I'll help you to remember them.

Author's note: 'Angel baby' and 'A Thousand Stars' are 1960s songs by Rosie and The Originals. Rosie Hamlin wrote 'Angel Baby' when she was only 14 years old. John Lennon often cited the song as his all-time favourite, and eventually recorded his own version.
Source: Wikipedia

AFTERNOON IN THE PARK

A mood ascends,
iron gate, silent plants.

I feed on the green,
like a savage beast.

Tin-coloured bin.
Wooden bench.
Tuna bagel to eat.

Sparrows picking crumbs,
from sunburnt grass,
burial ground of the wild.

Stony grail, empty chalice,
overgrown with lichen,
thistle and weed.

Underneath.
Dozing bum.

A trench, no shoes, no socks on his feet.

The noise from the traffic invades the calm,
kids run with sunshine on their breath.

My soul stretched bare, a kite riding high,
happiness exists, in this moment of time.

Found it suddenly, at the edge of the lake,
when the rowing boats came into sight.

Held on to it- hopeless effort,
like ice cream, melting in my hand.

GARDEN PATH

I can still remember,
how I skipped along the path,
not more than six, if that at all.

The grass knee-high,
pollinating,
the rays of the sun,
cathedral-like.

Through adventurous green,
jungle-land. The passing
of a butterfly, Admiral,
a mysterious find.

The apple tree, next to the wall,
still standing there today.
The grass is there, the same I suppose,

but to me, it all has changed.
Shrunken into insignificance,
like so many things nowadays.

Only a past-time memory, just
like myself, losing its meaning
on a distant summer's day.

WALKING TOWARDS THE WINDMILL

The ochre dust of the pathway
glistened as we stumbled along,
a trio of sunburnt women,
squinting our eyes tight.

The heat stung, we plunged on,
envisioning the conquered windmill,
a promise on the horizon,
quixotic Fata Morgana
of our holiday agenda.

Ignoring the dried-out land,
passing the tree-stem-like blossom
of the Aloe-Cactus, it was Ingrid,
the oldest, now dead,
who saw the dying bird first.

Feathers ruffled, wings spread
amongst the dust on the ground,
its glazed over eyes
looking up at the sky.

Someone with a gun should shoot him,
she said, her voice breaking,
put him out of his misery,
but we didn't have a gun and
there was no one else around.

We should have used a stone,
but we couldn't bring ourselves
to do that. Years later, with another
friend, on a walk, another dying bird,
we did just that. Both times, the only
consolation I came away with, was the
shade, granted by the nearby trees.

OF THE THINGS YOU DO NOT SEE

You don't see the way the moonlight
plays on the river, far away,
dark, flowing silently,
the air saturated with pine tree scent.
You don't see, how the stars
come out at night,
polish themselves,
sitting like diamonds on a velvet drape.
Nor, how in Africa, Antelopes
drink from a streamlet,
dried out almost completely
by the equator sun.
You could imagine, what the pyramids
look like:

Tourist guides leading camels along,
a whirl of sand playing around hoofs.
It is possible to imagine these things.
To imagine the banks of the river Nile,
fertile land, a farmer with a headscarf,
skin burnt. The sound of a machete
cutting grass, crickets chirping.

A flock of birds, taking off suddenly,
as if by secret command.
Or in Cairo-
walking down a dusty alleyway,
somebody singing in the afternoon,
slowly, attentively, melancholic,
in an inner courtyard, out of sight.

BOLOGNA

Stranded in a hotel room, next to the market halls,
woken up at six o'clock, - traders, shouting.

On our way to a breakfast bar, clumsily navigating,
freshly caught fish - their dead eyes turned towards heaven.

The Huzz and Buzz.
Suddenly, yellow limes, easy on the eye,
pushed along pork halves, the clamour of it all.

The wait between bread rolls and *Spremute*,
the blond woman behind the counter,
too proud to serve us.

People hastening by, on their way to work,
all dressed up, in the latest fashions.

We managed to find peace, eventually,
underneath some trees, sitting on a bench,

and Gudrun, who is unhappy,
until it is time to board the train home.

CERVO, ALASSIO

Sunburned houses owning hillsides,
like limpets glued to rocks.

Cypress trees, formidable sign posts.
Above us, caterpillar trains.

The sky hasn't changed its expression all day,
it remains Renaissance Blue.

Beach peddlers with their frippery and trinkets,
annoying extras on unspoiled sand.

Tourists melting on expensive sunbeds,
while romanticism fights with its protagonists.

In the evening, the waves lash onto the beach,
as if it is a competition.

Underneath the old coral church, San Giovanni,
a respite in the Café, gelato e acqua minerale.

History holds its breath for a moment:
Resurrecting Botticelli.

MEMORIES, DESTROYED

Only recently, I thought of the way she used to walk,
next to me, assured, confident and well-proportioned,
or so I thought, back then.

Black trousers, with matching, shiny top,
the way her long hair parted in the middle,
her trainers had just the right amount of wear and tear
to give them credibility, the same applied to her face.

Her speech was short, always to the point,
her manner was dismissive, carefree, cool.
Oh, how I envied her! She spent her afternoons
sitting in the front window at McDonald's, drinking Coke,
smoking cigarettes, the way we had seen it, at the movies.
You could do that back then, smoke inside restaurants,
and she was only fourteen.

When we went to the indoor swimming pool, she wore her black
Bikini, practiced her diving, and spoke about Florida.
She wanted to become a marine biologist, swim with dolphins.

When we came out of the baths, into the warm, summer's breeze
of the city, people carefree, laughing, she pretended to be
Farrah Fawcett Majors from Charlie's Angels,
her mind all golden, swinging hair,
the last sunrays of the afternoon dancing in it.
This was her Los Angeles, Hollywood.

She usually disappeared from my sight, when she was in that mood,
boarding a tram or a bus, with a casual and hastened *bye-bye*.
I knew she was happiest at times like that.
I've still got to do that ghastly math-work, see ya!

And I was happy myself, feeling, that I had witnessed something of great importance, like a glimpse of my grown-up future life, full of secrets and promise. The next day at school, she would tell me, how she'd picked up a portion of chips with ketchup and mayonnaise on her way home and spent the evening watching television, late into the night, then she'd done her homework, last minute, falling asleep over it. How lucky she was, that her mother worked at night.

I thought, *but we could have eaten those chips together.*

Over the school morning, her glamour tended to disperse, only to reappear when she sunned herself on the steps in the schoolyard, during intermission time, sometimes reading a music magazine.

Much later, I saw her again, by chance.
She was taking a tram into town.
She had aged before her time.
Her face tired, her eyes glazed over.

And I thought she'd be in Florida by now.
I was too shocked to talk to her.
I wish I hadn't seen her.
Florida and Los Angeles
were never quite the same.

SMALL TOWN, PASSING

As the midday train shoots past,
passenger's faces morph into
goldfish eyes in a glass bowl.

The stationmaster,
wrapped in his sou'wester,
passing wheels and wagons,
evoking wanderlust in his heart.

When the sunlight hits the
train's windows, it conducts an
epileptic staccato in his mind.

Just a station, not a stop.
Just a second, then gone,

before the land opens up...

Indigo mountains behind
a coke bottle on a rattling
side table, next to the
unfinished crossword puzzle
in the passenger's daily paper.

And two people asking:

What if we swapped places?

IT HAPPENED ON AN ORDINARY DAY

(on my side)

The bus shoots through **that** stretch of wood…

I always forget about the place - until I see it:
where the washing hangs out on plastic lines,
fluttering in the chilly November breeze.

Does it ever dry? I ask myself, as the pink trousers
and the bright blue pullover wave at me -
Unseasonal colours. Browns, beiges and oranges
are what one is supposed to wear this autumn.

I remember the UGG boots I bought last week.

As always, there are children playing outside,
no matter what the weather, a young girl
on a tricycle, her hair as black as her eyes,
a little boy, still in his pyjamas, stumbling along,
wearing winter boots, too big for his feet.

Is he crying? I can't tell. I imagine war zones,
unspeakable horrors, frozen in tiny faces,
unmovable masks, the sound of shelling,
dust and debris, one arm missing, or a leg.

I turn away, towards the soothing green of
dense pine woods - think of something else-
like upcoming Christmas preparations.
I overhear two elderly ladies, sitting two rows
ahead of me: 'What an eyesore! They should
work for a living!'

I remember the satellite dishes on top of the
grey buildings - where are they pointing?
What news do they pick up? From what country?

The overflowing garbage bins, the tossed shopping
cart - yes, it is an eyesore, but probably nothing
compared to what those eyes saw.

I sigh as the bus stops to take a couple of youths aboard,
dressed in denim and black sneakers, oblivious to it all,
I-pods in their ears, escaping into their own world -
and who can blame them! The bus turns, goes overland.
The sun shines through my side of the window, warming
it up, lulling me into sleep, helped along by the monotonous

sound of the diesel engine –

(on her side)

till voices wake me up.
I can't understand them at first, a face comes into focus,
trees outside the window. I forget where I am, only for
a moment - then I recognize my husband, his dark hair,
the scar across his face, a mirror of his soul -

and I remember: 'Nan' - half her face blown off, as
they pulled us away from her, how we ran through rubble.
The door opens, and my son comes in, still in his
pyjamas, one boot has come off his foot, his sister follows,
clinging to that tricycle, she hasn't smiled since **that** day.

'We've missed the bus', my husband says, 'now we'll
have to walk to the shops, come on.' I remember
the bus. I see it every morning. It rushes past at
eleven and there is a woman sitting in the window,
right at the back. She has red hair and wears a black coat.

Somehow she looks terribly familiar, but that can't be…

COVER THEIR CAGES

Cover their cages, birds only sing in the dark.

Maybe it is because they're scared, the way one whistles in the dark.

Ruffle their rainbow-coloured feathers, birds of paradise.

Shimmering in the dusty sunlight of some stuffy living room.

Cover their cages, birds only sing in the dark.

People sing in the dark, whenever they're scared. Or do they whistle?

Suffocate the sunshine, we know what's to be done.

Split the clean from the unclean. It'll only take a moment.

And if it hurts, heaven is their reward. Hold all this, safe and sound.

There is some distant singing, echo of the jungle's call. This is some strange religion.

Hand and foot perch claw-like. Teeth gnashing. Excruciating. Can I hear her sing?

This is an ancient ritual. No one can hear you scream. Those fabric wings won't fly anymore.

It is an ancient ritual. Cover their cages, birds only sing in the dark.

Author's note:
This poem's theme is about locking up and controlling something you love, thus destroying its beauty in the process. Depriving a bird of the freedom and joy of flying, its true nature. Even the clipping of a wing, to prevent escape. It is also an allegory for the same treatment a lot of women (and men) still have to suffer, in the form of restrictive clothes and the horrors of female and male genital mutilation, all in the name of religion and ancient customs. I would like to see this poem as a reminder for empathy with the vulnerable, in whatever form it may cross our path.

GUIDE DOGS FOR THE BLIND

Lopsided frame of a man, hair curly black-grey,
out of square, like the creature at his feet, same colour of fur,
leaning against his washed-out Jeans legs.

Chumming up, mid-stream, to festive shoppers,
Christmassy pedestrian zone, mid-town decorations aglow,
the clink-clunk of coins in the collecting tin.

Black Labrador drawing, on a red, round box,
overemphasizing simple-hearted hope of visual deliverance,
amongst a multisensory ocean of impressions.

If only skill might be this easily exchanged,
like trading cards from our childhood, valued and discarded
at our heart's content, life, you are never that simple.

Authors note: Inspired by the poem 'A Mite Box' by Seamus Heaney

INLET

The way the paint flakes off the hull of a propped-up boat,
this is how I feel today.
The sand a damp cloth underneath my feet, shifting my equilibrium
this way, that way,
ready to throw me off balance any time.

Yet, clinging to the denseness, the omnipresence of the sky,
with its towering grey clouds,
almost tangible, as my hands make believe they can touch them,
while I think of you.

MISCONCEPTION

We drive along the coastal road,
tiny dots on the map of life-
like fish would swim along the shore:

Its meandering loops installing them
with a sense of destiny. Dreaming
of depth, currents, the promise of adventure.

Unaware of the fishermen's fleet-
men in dark teal sou'westers,
cursing the weather as they earn a living,
screaming their thoughts into the breeze.

My eyes follow them, as they throw
their patched-up nets overboard,
waves swallowing them up,
while their boats ride the tide.

At home we sit down for a cup of tea,
the spindrift running down our shoes,
as we open a tin of canned mackerel,
spreading its content evenly on warm toast.

INNER LANDSCAPES

DON QUIXOTE IS DEAD

It was at his funeral, that I remembered.

We could see the windmill from our attic window.
Quixotic Mirage on the horizon of a dried-out plane.
Endless land of wheat fields, stretching and
yearning into adolescence, like the five of us.

Excited, racing towards it, conquering on rusty, low-framed
bicycles, mile after mile, unattainable Chimera, glistening
in feverish August heat, full of promise and purpose,
like our ambitions, the ones we'd lose, in the years ahead.

Back then, hours extended into eternity,
moods formed cocoons for us to nestle in,
the way mammals hibernate: cosy, comforted,
unperturbed, with a secret code embedded
in their DNA.

He had found a stick along the path,
punching the air with it, riding ahead,
breeze on his face, hair and spit
flying backwards, as he yelled:
I'm Don Quixote! Watch out you stupid
windmill! I'm Don Quixote, here I come!

Don Quixote has been dead for six days now.
The sharp blades of life's windmills have finally
won the battle. I guess his suit of armour
wasn't that strong after all. As I listen to the priest's
monotonous monologue, I'm thinking to myself:

When words are not enough,
all else will fail -
the blind stumble in a haze of light.

THE EMPTY PLACE

*Where has she gone? Her place is empty now.
But she did once upon a time, merely
physically speaking, displace space, and
the air around her. I admit it was a fair exchange,
air in, air out, one calls it breathing - until it stops —*

*But all the same, there was something like
a displacement of space, where she stood,
or walked, or sat, or lay. I know, I'm repeating
myself, but it is important to clarify this now,
once and for all.*

That's what he said to me, the other day,
when we were sitting together, drinking
a cup of tea, something special nowadays,
in these times of epidemic restrictions.
And then he said to me:

*These thoughts are my gift to you,
because you have to write something,
or want to*, he says, as he sees me raise
my hand in protest. *Still*, he says, *it's the
same for a poet, isn't it?*

He's right about that.

And he already knows my answer to his question,
but he doesn't want to hear it, or believe it.
Well, he **wants to really**, but he just can't,
not completely, although, recently…

Deep down he believes this after all:
That she is now in a beautiful place, her
soul that is, or her astral body, or whatever
you want to call it, and that she is fine
where she is now, and that she laughs like
she used to laugh, in the old days, when
she was still here, to displace space.

Then, he told me again how much he
envies me, because of my certainty,
because I have a sense for these things
and are able to establish contact,
on several occasions, with the dog
and my mother, because her spirit walked
next to me on the beach, that of my mother,
and because she told us not to be sad,
my father and I, for she was feeling
so well, now that her pain was gone.

And then I said, *but Sylvie's spirit
stood right next to you, in the garden,
by the tall fir trees, next to the stacked wood,
where the light is so special, and you said,
that she even held your hand, and that you had
felt that quite distinctly. The other day…*

Yes, he admits.
*But then I cannot accept this
gift*, I insist. *After all, it's your idea, your
story, and you are a writer yourself.*

Yes, but not like you, he said, *you
publish your work as well.*
Occasionally, I said, *that's true,
but only now and then.*

Nevertheless, he said –

OK. Then this here is for Sylvie,
wherever she is, and it is also for Les,
who is still crying, after all those years,
who still loves her so much, and who
is still hoping to see her again, one day.

Who still hopes so much

DREAMWALK

There is a feeling to rediscover,
gazing outside my window-

Streetlamp shines its milky light.
Summer night,
drunken with the smell of blossom,
a hint of promise colours the night.
I recall the memory,
of a recurring dream,
full of mysterious variations.
There is endlessness
in this feeling-
a dreamwalk down empty streets.
On and on, downhill,
through dim-lit housing estates
and unlit building sites.
The memory of a train,
that stopped,
in the middle of the night.
The loneliness,
of a cold autumn night,
felt as a small child,
walking next to my mother,
holding onto her hand,
guided only, by the light of a lonely streetlamp.

THE ETERNAL PUZZLE

But now he is able to perceive, behind her mask,
fragile porcelain, notices how the old façade
is disintegrating,
being the only one, who is able to see it,
as if that was a sign.

Chiselled core of marble,
naked torso in a museum, on display,
for greedy eyes to gaze at,
exposed to the audacity of stranger's hands,
arms and legs broken off, gaunt and mottled,
lying at the base of its pedestal.

He picks up her limbs,
places them on a wooden shelf,
behind a red velvet curtain, one by one,
in the attic over his chamber.

Midday, he finds her head at an
antique's market, sitting between
old trinkets, her lips dried out,
eyelids closed.

Carefully, he wraps her head into
a silk scarf, tenderly, cautious,
his trembling hands touching
her countenance.

From the museum
he steals her torso,
under the cover of night,
only the green haze of the
emergency light to guide him.

While he assembles the pieces,
standing at the ocean shore,
she suddenly opens her eyes,
watery, like the colour of the sea.

THE LAST TIME I SAW YOUR FACE

was almost a foreboding,
as the autumn foliage
strain-hardened the ambiguity
of our smiles, splitting
a mood clean. That moment
when a rifle shot exploded
into the roughness of the
terrain, undergrowth
silenced, tree-trunks
giving birth to an inkling,
and a bird of prey abandoned
a half-eaten carcass, falling
unrecognisably at our feet.

AS MAN AS HORSE

to remember a time, a place, or a person, he said to me,
it's all the same, everyday tapestry coming together,
a jigsaw puzzle, kowtowing eternity, falling through
the cracks of our emotional landscape, like the way
an idea skims backwards, remembering itself,
a breeze sung to tighten the treeline of our souls,
jerking a mood into place, an unfinished intention,
a refurbished room, a racehorse in full flight,
all four hooves airborne, levitating split-second,
the idea of ground conquered, Pegasus ad infinitum,
gravity-vanishing act, sky reclaimed, never to return
to our earthly plane, a shot fired from a rifle,
put out of its misery, the kind thing to do,
once the back spine is broken.

I WILL DIE ON A WEDNESDAY

I will die on a Wednesday,
to the chimes of the midday bell,
as the children run onto the playground,
carefree, wind in their hair.

I will die on a Wednesday,
as the sparrows sing,
underneath the old oak tree,
next to the park bench.

I will die on a Wednesday,
as the first flowers of spring
blossom in the meadow,
next to the small stream,

and the scent of freshly baked bread
will enter my room,
through the window, you left open.

I will die on a Wednesday.

I will lie on top of my bed,
while a breeze plays with the curtains,
and it will be spring,

but you will not cry,
because you know,
the last thing I saw,
was the small bird,
in the house opposite,
who in an unwatched moment,
escaped its prison,
to fly into the bright afternoon.

Author's note: Inspired by the poetry of Cesar Vallejo (1892-1938) and Juan Ramon Jimenez (1881-1958), in particular by the poems 'Black stone on top of a white stone/Piedra negra sobre una piedra blanca' by Vallejo, and 'The final journey/El viaje definitivo' by Jimenez.

NEW MORNING

Just like yesterday
the crows are resting
on the roof of the old
spire, as if they own
this village.

The fields, still silent,
with their cover of
morning mist, the river
asleep in its sandy bed.

Finally, people have left this place.

Innocence has returned.

CHANCE MEETING

He said we live in the latter days,
I thought of the homeless, lost.
I saw an empty beer can, squeezed,
on the path, a dustbin tossed,
I said an inner prayer,
of miracles to come,
more on the verge of
dreams to share, with those
who might still care.

The bus drove off,
the moment gone,
a puddle left behind,
where only then,
a moment ago,
a rainbow
tried to
shine.

ESCAPOLOGY

There sure is more than meets the eye,
a whole army that wants to sequester,
and what it advertises, so smoothly
puts forward, is always bigger than life itself.
The insolence smarts - so hollow it is -
Villains, passing us their sweet, poisonous cup.

Don't fear the maladroit Greek philosophers,
it is the eloquent conquistadors, who laugh and sing,
while they ram the lance into the bull's side,
you have to fear.

To avert danger in the face of such charades,
far-sightedness will master faith in the
inconspicuous, unlikely trove, born of fire,
- white heat - a thousand degrees -

Handcuffs will simply melt away.

NEWSROOM@HORROR.COM

What is this desperation? Endless horror carved in ice,
more screams of people's anguish, plasma frames of our minds.
Somewhere, someone's always crying, rubble piles up meter-high,
horrifying infotainment, and a thousand more will die.
Rebels fighting mad dictators - children play with loaded guns,
while bullet-proof reporters, get blown up on the run.
Angry, deceived pensioners, take their life, or to the streets.
A violent mob kicks heads in, that have fallen to their feet.
You can sense a rising danger, peace - not welcome anymore,
disillusion eats our dreams up, God knows what will be the score.
Heartless greed destroys the planet, poisons water, kills off bees,
helpless animals get used up, lying tortured at our feet.
No wonder we're all cynical, burning up on society's fringe,
our bleeding souls depressive, sanity hanging on a hinge.

ANGER

We sat in silence, restrained
by suburban subordination,
inferior satellites in I-pod
and coffee-to-go-ness land

2nd and 53rd row material,
we managed to crawl out of
the gutter, muted by our
knowledge of life's dreary

soundtrack screaming in
our ears, exhausting the
spirit in loops, inhaling
fearful desperation as we

sat in silence, emptied of
hopeful efforts, along an
endless future in a tiny
single room,
life-support-system
for high-flyers.

First published in Aberration Labyrinth Magazine, March 2013

BELISHA-CINDY

Semi-detached next to Belisha beacon, Cindy on Common Crescent can help.
Just call her 'Belisha-Cindy', for so does everybody else.

Two-hundred pounds heavy, you don't fuck around with this girl- no way.
Could've been a stunner, weren't it for ciggies and alc, that dragged her looks away.

The girl's forty-seven, so give her a break. Got her own problems, okay?
Not letting on though, just cares about others - more than you can say.

Her best mate's called Rob, not your textbook bloke, he knows 'bout life, been through it all. Got a brother up north and a wife who's with another, two boys of eleven, freckled twin pair.

He never talks about them, just cries night and day, and drinks their absence away.

Cindy's a clairvoyant, for a packet of fags, she'll read you your cards and your palms,
and it ain't true, all that talk 'bout her drinking a bottle of vodka a day.

I've seen people on that, they don't look like her: hair shiny, tinted and long,
fingernail extensions, knitted jumper - her signature look from hell.

Visitors roosting in the front room, if not collecting their dole,
you'll find them sitting at Cindy's place,
cuppa in hand, telly on full blare.
Don't need an appointment, just knock on her door,
the beacon's blinking all day.

VACANCY

It was Jenny who said the place was haunted first.
Got it from her brother Alfi, that busted, tope bastard.
It's the vacant factory up Hill Street she bragged, so
'nomen est omen' Frenemy Fran joined in, like she's
so into Jen's dude, it's gross, but she's like, *so what?*
I've been there on me own, no big deal you pussies
And she's all super-size in the right places, real scary,
that's why Jenny ignored it and the rest were like,
yeah, cool.

We went there Friday; Fran, Jen, Jack, Meg,
Mark, meself and Jess. Getting well buzzed up
before midnight, snapshot-shitting, and all that.
Jess getting flamed again, with Fran hollering
Shut up you victim! and Mark who looks like a
Brotox almost hitting her, when we heard that
mega-eerie sound and I almost pissed myself.

Rumour has it, a man snuffed it there, three years
ago, don't know if it's true, cause people talk crap
all the time. They say there's a satanic circle, that's
sacrificing cats, plus this creepy red stain on the floor,
right next to the window - I saw it when Jenny shone
her torchlight, but it could've been just rust.

Then Meg started taking pix again, and her flashlight
got us well worked up and I think I saw some'ing
in one of the corners, close to the ceiling, and Jack
saw it too. Even Fran screamed, which NEVER happens,
so, we knew it was real.

I HATE this sort of thing, when I'm somewhere and I'm
shit tired and I just wanna be home and cuddle up in
bed and drink my cocoa and tell mum she's WELL SAD.
But this is so PEAK, I mean, with this ghost-thing, it's
like that REALLY cool American TV series, they haven't even
shot yet, and we're all in it, it's just nobody's watching it, man.

And hey, it's not as if we were all wavey, not like
we normally are. So, what 'appens is, we make a run
for it, and then we laugh like we're a bunch of wallads.

Later we take a look at Meg's mobile pix and all you can
see is this murky mist and that's probably just dust, but
when those losers ask on Monday how it was, we just say

ACE!

EQUINOX

The green sprawling underneath my feet,
resembling vintage glass. A cracked surface,
air bubbles trapped in an icy mirror.
I advance, evoking the rest of my path.

I know, it doesn't matter anymore,
the equinox has been traversed,
everything from now on
will be received as
an unexpected gift:

The yellow of the colza blossom,
its sweet scent stunning my senses.
The calls of the cream-coloured cows,
grazing underneath ancient oak trees.

All expectations have been drowned.
My feet drag on, robot-like. My heart
still dreams: Point Zero. Eye of the
storm. Land of OZ. I can hear your
breath.

INSIDE THE OBSERVATORY

I never think about the stars,
unless I see them on TV,
in some spooky Astro-Show,
with a geek, sporting a beard.

I'd rather roam my inner space,
a familiar kind of depth,
all there, within my reach:
Black Holes, Blue Moon, my death.

A supernova to burn my soul.
A solar storm from pole to pole.
A milky-way to rendezvous.
A wormhole for the crew.

Saturn's rings are spinning mad,
by the time I lie in bed,
my thoughts are going round and round,
within my cloudy head.

This is my Star Wars, Enterprise,
Endeavour and Dark Star,
you see, my Galaxy, is really
not that far.

One day the two of us might meet,
in some low-gravity place,
if only you would join me there,
within my inner space.

DESTINY, REVISITED

I followed your footsteps
along the Boulevard of Broken Dreams.

Listened to their soft echo
along the steaming concrete's surface.

You almost turned around,
aware of my presence in the shadows, lingering.

Your head inclined to the left,
a smile playing around the corner of your mouth.

As a convertible cruised by,
the palm trees gently swayed in the breeze.

HIGH-WAY-LOVE-PRAYER

So, I go to see that voodoo priest, steaming hot French
Quarter, Moss Dolls, Skull Bracelets, Bourbon Street,
New Orleans Skeletons, that Zombie House, he calls
a home, sitting on an Alligator chair, can you imagine?
I pay him twenty dollars, then he mumbles this spell for me:

*'Spellbound future, do behold her, as she begins to tumble,
let her dwell forever, inside your pink-skin-shelter, embracing
fruit-juice-jellyness, within a plastic wrapper, time-fractals,
skulduggery-symphony, jackpot in a slot machine.'*

And I swear, and I sweat, and I curse, and my heart, it bleeds,
and you never wanted to come here, and my best friend is YOU,
so, I'm borrowing Darkling's Chapel, and to hell with speed limits,
I'll get that Raven Tattoo, in black and violet and blue, on the back
of my shoulder. I'll switch off that fucking cruise control and I'll
speed into a star-studded night and howl at the bloody blue moon,
singing songs I don't even know, lullabying our future-life-ghosts,
and I'll cry, and I'll fly, and I'll dream, and I'll will it all into existence'
I'll voodoo it, if it's the last goddamn thing I do.

THE PLACE EVERYONE KNOWS

Memories, lying in wait,
like a drawer full of
electronic waste.

The recollection of a scent,
pink bubblegum,
pale plastic flowers,
in the seating area
of an American Diner.

The Motel room with
its brown corduroy sofa,
orange ornaments on 70s wallpaper,
a mud green telephone and
the hum of the air conditioning.

We fill up our paper cups with
Ice and Coke from the machine
located on the landing, then drive on,
down endless, conifer lined
highways, underneath a blazing
August sun.

Where we'll end up-
We do not know
When we'll arrive-
Is uncertain

A German Version of this poem was first published in 2010
with 'Bibliothek Deutschsprachiger Gedichte', München

ONE AFTERNOON

The afternoon prepares
to remember itself, as

I sit in my kitchen
that has seen better days,

a feeling steals up
on me, of those times

I spent with my friend,
talking the world into place,

giving it face,
softening its sharpness.

It's just coincidence
that my glance falls

upon the glass, she
once gave to me, out

of a mood, back then,
one afternoon.

SOUL-CHRYSALIDES

There, underneath that southern cross,
endless, immense wideness of a
star-studded sky, when the desert
fox runs across an imaginary line,
plants himself in infant's hearts the
moment they are born, to tear and pull
at life's elastic strings and cords, merciless,
until they won't stretch any further, to
catapult the spirit into whatever form
it may enter. Kachina dancers have
collected you, eternal spirits, across
old prairie-land.

AT PEACE, AT LAST

Who listens to confessions made in church?
The child that's all innocence and praise.
The priests amongst their wooden benches,
who dream of stone-faced angels.

Years of cryptic signs misread, vitas lost their
veritas, with mortgaged hearts and broken glass,
now is the time to breach the charm, the speech
misplaced, the guilt is real, an echo of the past.

Drive onwards then, leaving a scar, the garbage
in the car. Across the border, another corner,
happiness afar. Silence, mountains, trees and
stars, lonely heart amongst the thieves, you are

at peace, at last.

DEAD MAN'S BENCH

Sat down on dead man's bench today,
as the dandelions and the daffodils
were spread around the ground.

Watching the newborn lambs
graze in the field ahead;
The soothing sun on their woollen backs.

Missing the tobacco scent of his cigarette,
the bottle of beer, the way he played
with the dog, as we talked for a while.

Weltschmerz in his voice.
Never knew his name.
Wasn't important.

He's gone over a year now.
The snow that covered his grave
has melted, all that's left
is the bench we used to sit on.

Dead man's bench.

WRONG TURN

After three hours, she starts to rename
the familiar while spaciousness is
playing hopscotch with her mind.
Approaching headlights start radiating
hoodoo, so, she invents memories
that form a line of defence:

Sunny Summer Sundays…

Merry-Go-Round Horses…

Red-White Fabric Tinsel…

Soda-Popsicle Ice Creams…

Pink Bubble Gum Sentiments…

But reality is relentless:

National-forest-reclusiveness turning into
wolf's-playground-territory, giving birth
to a sophomoric Grimm's tale:
Windscreen de-ice-skulduggery
liquefying her anxiety
a paroxysm unfurling some deep
recess in her mind - she is so past the point where
she can get away with reason. The landscape comes
at her, like jagged and shifting rocks, incrementally
imposing themselves, encroaching, dark fireflies in
BLACK BLOCK LETTERS.
Shadow-world occurrences, some grim reaper-
it's like sitting at a rickety wooden table, dinner
sliding off, catcalls from the past, the rocky slope
of her life, coming to a complete standstill in a
ditch near the M6.

IN LANCASHIRE

He was last seen around midnight,
up north, in some grubby nightclub.
Like a cliché - they found his mobile
In a ditch. Forerunner model of the
I-phone one's supposed to have.
She keeps tormenting herself, if it would've
made any difference, a longer battery LIFE-
Grotesque analogy

She had said **NO** when he'd begged her for the newest model,
but the question is pointless, as is watching that game show,
now that he's no longer there any more, to holler the answers.
She sits at her kitchen table, touching its wax cloth,
turning it into a cerecloth, underneath the earth-brown
Denby Teapot, with its Typhoo Teabag, causing a maelstrom
for her sorrows to drown in.
Only nineteen!
The voice of the newsreader mocks her LOVE-
As he lists his clothes. And then she asks herself:
*WHY does her son's leather jacket look like a copy of the life they had together?
And why does she suddenly remember the blue Pigeon Egg he'd found when he
was only five years old?*
Time is a bastard!
It opens up a crevice reaching
all the way to the other side of the universe,
or to his room upstairs- It's the same.
They say that a forty-six-year-old man
is helping the police with their inquiries
and it takes a moment to register with her,
what that means, for her first impulse is to think
That's kind of a stranger to help
but then she sees him, handcuffed, head
shielded by the hand of a policeman, being
pushed into one of those multicoloured police-
cars and she thinks to herself *how modern
they look. Those cars. Nowadays.*

They finally find him in the ten o'clock news.
In some muddy field in Lancashire.
She muses, how she's never been to Lancashire and the fact that her son's been there, even only as a corpse, installs a kind of solace in her. She doesn't know where it comes from, but she knows she can't let it go. Never wants to let it go. And she mumbles *Lancashire* to herself. All day long. All through the night. As if it was a magic word. A kind of spell. Something to bring him back. Eventually. One day. And when a neighbour calls or friends come round, she says to them:
It's all right, he's just in Lancashire!

THE 79

does not go to City Centre anymore,
it just rushes past that grey old brick wall –

I try not to notice, sitting in the aisle seat,
away from the window, leaving the space empty,
like for an absent guest of honour, something
about the way his physicality redistributed
the air's molecules, a moveable mausoleum,
until a freckled schoolgirl wants to sit there,
pushing herself past, heaving a heavy satchel
close to my face, missing the nose by an inch,
Sorry, Mrs, doesn't quite cut it, but I let it go,
numbed by the mundaneness of it all, but then
I reconsider, ponder how he would have liked it,
in a kinky kind of way, the girl's thighs touching
the seat's surface, the way the naked skin of her legs
gets caressed by the red velvety feel of the fabric,
the girl's breath fresh with spearmint gum, her hair
releasing a green apple shampoo scent.

Her school bag weighs heavy, so did his coffin.
Six strong men were required, uneven shoulders,
I wanted to cry, but couldn't, as if a lump of clay,
full of moisture, was clogging my food or windpipe,
like the handful they made us throw onto the casket's lid.

It has rained all day, and the sunshine, now streaming
through the bus window, seems absurd, like the call
of a mockingbird, in the wasteland of the rest of my life.

The seventy-nine does not go to City Centre anymore.
It does for everybody else, but not for me. My body
remains seated, but my soul gets off at the stop called

Cemetery.

AD INFINITUM

I imagine how he sits down for breakfast:
Eyes already tired of this world, hands,
liver spots and bulging veins.
He drinks orange juice and coffee
while his life story re-enters his face,
shapes it for the coming day,
smooths out the skin's surface
one could almost touch,
but shies away,
out of fear, it might break.

His parents worked hard,
those times are gone.
A faded sepia print in his restless heart.
I can almost smell the childhood corridors
he walked down, the burning coal on a winter's day,
that steaming canalisation, the pong of a vegetable stew
competing with floor polish.

There is illness in the air.
His spectacles hold bad news at bay - and love.
But tenderness seeps through, treads carefully.
Now he turns a page of the morning paper,
meaningless to the core of his being.
Turning and turning

ad infinitum.

WAKE OF THE DEAD

The surface grey, potato peels,
the garden, a lost continent.
More books to dust, no air to breathe,
the room, a tomb in space.
Curtains pale, so fragile the cup
- the last meal he took.

This picture does not breathe anymore,
the grandfather clock has stopped.
Last letter received a week ago,
'Apples galore, make pie,
can you bring some wood?'

The flame's gone out,
will not come back,
a stroke was all it took.

THE ARRIVAL

I'll put my foot on the doorstep.

If I'll go ahead, the house won't be the same.
I'll breathe its space into the cavern of my chest.

I'll attempt what legions have tried before.
To place the capstone on a lifelong rehearsal:

Badly fitting Macintosh, hanging skew-whiff
on his shoulder, unhinged by life's blow of fate,
unapt cover for this delicate frame.

The old house could tell you
stories, the last one, still on
display. The space inside is
endless, but a radio keeps guard.
Trees form a perfect
picture frame. A middle-aged
lady walks her dog, thighs bulky,
access luggage. In my jacket
pocket, moist fingers have
crumbled my airplane ticket,
the taxi now a memory of smells,
the drivers' crucifix dangling voodoo-
like, red brakes flashing, as he drives
around the corner. It is then, that I
decide to unlock the front door.

GRANDMOTHER

Yesterday I thought of you.
You were in the green of the pine tree,
next to the old railway station.

As the first snow of winter fell, I found you downtown,
in the promise of a bargain handbag.

I saw you midweek, in the two middle-aged women,
standing shoulder by shoulder at the street corner,
faces grim, holding up their watchtower magazines.

I could hear your whisper when a tram shot past,
and a gust of wind played with a lonely plastic bag.

I could see you crystal clear, in your favourite armchair,
the one with the lace covers, in that overheated room,
next to the canary cage, always open, except at night.

In the crossword puzzle, delicately filled in,
with that Biro of yours, assured.

I swear I could hear your footsteps behind me,
that morning in November, when I went to the zoo
and stood next to the lion's cage.

Later, I definitely saw your face, in the upstairs window,
of the Chinese restaurant, the one you loved so much;
You sat there, with your hair of silvery white, and smiled.

Then, one rainy afternoon, when I ordered coffee and cake,
in that old-fashioned place, I just knew you sat next to me.
I could smell your perfume.

But one place I'd never find you,
is by that grave with the weathered sandstone.

That's the reason I never go there.
I'm sure you understand.

MY TREASURE WITHOUT COMPARE

And if all the stars in the night sky would
unite to light up my path, they could not
compare with the light you shine, eclipsing
them all, a heart full of gemstones, your
treasure chest, sparkling, twinkling,
a thousand colours, no rainbow could ever possess.

And if all the flowers in the meadow, would
send me the sweetest of scent, they still would
be no comparison to the sweetness my heart feels
as soon as you are near.

And if all the waves of the ocean, would ebb to-and-fro
for me, seagulls screeching above in the sky, singing their
Lullaby to a clear blue sky, the most beautiful seashells
delighting my heart, they would be no match if we were apart.

And if springtime's sparrows would sing their romantic
song, around the park benches at Montmartre, circling
Sacre Coeur, and turtledoves would coo on tiny house roofs,
Oh! What good would it do, if you weren't sitting next to me?

So let this treasure stay with me forever, for what
could all the world and its gold bring me, if I had
not you, and the sailing boats on the horizon would
not take my love ashore.

DAUGHTER NATURE

She carries solace inside
herself, like cut flowers
feed on blood in a vase.

Timeless and placeless,
can't locate her origin –
obnoxious form.

Her bony, long fingers,
bark-stripped branches
on a dying winter tree.

With hair, that wants to
remind herself of seaweed.
Slimy strands, afloat a forgotten
ocean.

Her distant cry, a seismic sensation
in my shipwrecked heart –
cryptic sign of something
lost.

A flock of seagulls gathers
around her, circle of ether-like birds,
emitting an indigo glow.

My mood follows them,
as the fizzy-topped waves
hit the unspoiled edge
of the ocean's shore.

FEAR MADE OF FISH

A lake so green, it might just as well be grass,
while fish eat the last sun rays of gold.

It is all about hiding and catching,
the furtive wait beneath a leaf.

Painfully plain to see.

How tiny mouths gasp for air,
orifices transgressing the element.

I watch while cold air stings sharp
in my lungs,
revealing an ancient fear
I cannot decode.

Caught up in a place in time
when I was still in awe;
the world a mocking song,
playing gently with the moods
of my intangible mind.

PROMENADE WITH MAGRITTE

Looking down from Manet's balcony,
the path can be well described,
as it meanders through the Land of Love:

Past the Equestrienne in the forest,
tête-à-tête with the relics of shadows,
further into the empire of lights,
where the enlightened one resides
within the house of secrets.

The eternal evidence bears witness,
to the tree of knowledge,
and high up, in the clouds,
floats the castle in the Pyrenees,
above a sea of infinity.

Had the arrow of Zeno
not shown us the way,
we would hardly have discovered
the pipe next to the lady's shoe.

And even if the scale of fire
seemed a little strange to us,
we would by no means have
wanted to miss the winged
gentleman in his tailcoat,
on the bridge.

Only the look of the lion
made us wonder a little,
but since this wasn't an apple,
we didn't give the matter
much thought.

Inspired by the surrealistic paintings of the Belgian painter
Rene Magritte (1898-1967)

DE CHIRICO'S DREAM

Across the immenseness of the desolate, deserted square,
he promenades alone, towards the neoclassical colonnade.

In the distance
a steam-train paints
cotton candy clouds
into the loneliness
of this afternoon.

And while he circles the sleeping statue,
his gaze rests upon the distant figures,
standing at the base of the giant tower.

May it be,
that they are aware of melancholia's secret;

But,
they haven't noticed the poet's departure.

Author's note: I dedicate this poem to one of my favourite painters,
the metaphysical surrealist Giorgio de Chirico, 1888-1978

THE KEEPERS OF TIME

The guardian and his apprentice
are walking across the Plaza
in the midday sunshine,
that sends its sparks
into the infinity
of future hearts.

In the distance of the summers' heat
a lonely train sounds its whistle.
They watch, as the white steam
paints candyfloss clouds into
the blue silence of the sky.

The guardian glances at the
old clock, in the square,
which is placed up high in
the round stone tower
with the small windows.

He nods to his apprentice
-it is time to go-
He takes out the key
he has kept in his
velvety coat all day.

The iron key makes
a grinding sound
as it is turned
in the ancient lock.

The staircase up the tower
is steep with
sandstone steps.
Until they reach the sky
it does take a while.

They cast their eyes
across the land, sprawling
underneath them.
The big hands of the
clock at an arms-length.

It is almost twelve now,
but still some minutes to go.
They are just in time again
to stop time running out.

And as they grab the
cast-iron pointers
with all the effort
they can manage
another day is saved.

Underneath them,
in the town square,
nobody notices
that their sunshine
is made of
golden crystals.

FANTASIA FAUNUS

Standing next to *Cel* at the funeral pyre
of past future hopes and dreams,

embedded organic clock ticking away in the caverns
of the rotting carcasses that came into being

at point zero of our lives - like the motionless
marble statues, asleep in some forgotten

Italian palazzo, next to a lost and overgrown
garden; The sweet smell of acacia and cypress

conspiring with *Aradia*, bewitching summer's crickets,
a cacophony, life's soundtrack, wake-up call pending.

*Go away, let me dwell in sweet slumber, sensual
sensation, dreaming our perfect world into endless existence.*

Receiving a veil of waterdrops from the fountain's mouth
nestling on our androgynous face, *Anteros* witnessing

the birth of the eternal hermaphrodite.

Authors note
Mythical figures, featured in the poem:

Faunus is the Roman and Italian horned god of woodlands, plains and fields. He symbolizes love and reveals the future in dreams and voices.

Cel is the Italian god of death and the underworld.
Aradia is an Italian witch goddess. Her mother, Diana, ordered her to come to earth and to teach humanity magic. She is a lunar spirit, also known as the moon goddess.

Anteros is the Italian, Roman and Greek god of love and passion, specifically, the god of mutual love.

A *hermaphrodite* is an organism, that has reproductive organs normally associated with both male and female sexes. *Hermaphroditos* was the Greek, winged Love-God of hermaphrodites and effeminate men. He was the son of Hermes and Aphrodite. Source: Wikipedia

TIME

I trusted it with my life, as it hobbled along
on crutches next to me, its incapacitated walk
giving nothing away.

I should have known better.
It was a sign of things to come.
Like umbrellas embracing the rain-
their cheerful colours, substitutes
for the sun.

Time – on some afternoons I get a glimpse of it,
as it outruns me, rushes around a corner, always
two steps ahead.

By the grocery store, for example,
where the kids buy their sweeties and comics;
Running, screaming, open/wide sky
on their breaths, freedom found in an instant.

Or at the bakery – on display in the form of
tiny pastel coloured cupcakes. Vermicelli on top of
sumptuous sugar frosted icing. Mouthwateringly so.

I thought I had plenty of time left,
but I lost it somehow,
gradually, without noticing.

I guess it must have happened
one Thursday afternoon,
between a bus ride into town,
and a walk down the lane.

But occasionally I get a glimpse of it.

Last week, I felt its presence downtown
in the huge bookstore. I saw it hiding between
the international newspapers, the ones that tell you
about the world, the one I used to belong to,
once upon a time.

Not that long ago.

NIGHT FLIGHT

It was during those nights, that I couldn't sleep.

My life was too bright. But I only understood this

years later.

They say we need the shadows,

the darkness as a contrast.

Like bats, who fly in the night,

with an inner compass to navigate our melancholy,

or our fears. Something to push us forward,

towards the continent of the Unspeakable.

HOUR OF DELIVERANCE

My gaze rests upon the veil
that prophets dared to raise.
My feet walk along the path
that wise men came to praise.

Memories of future days
with magic light sustained,
are gathering within my soul
with insight to be gained.

I gravitate more to the point
where silence takes on face,
which surfaces within myself
up from a hidden place.

As my gaze rests on the roses,
growing in my heart,
the sweetest torment liberates,
and tears my soul apart.

UNNOTICED

Last house in the street.

Dim lantern,
leading the way.

Low fog over the river.

A Passer-by
stops momentarily.

Old church bell,
strikes just once.

Nighttime,
with transparent layers.

Last house in the street.

A shadow glides around your corner-
Unnoticed by your inhabitants.

ABOUT THE AUTHOR

Susanne Rowell, born in Düsseldorf, Germany, writer, painter, and photographer, has published English and German poetry and short stories, online, in print magazines and anthologies.